Robyn Hood

And Other Stories

Marlys Addison

Bishop Publishing

Dedication

These stories are dedicated to my daughter, for whom I fight to make the world a better place.

Contents

Acknowledgments

No big project is created alone. I couldn't write if my family, friends, coworkers, and acquaintances hadn't been such rich, engaging people.

Robyn Hood

Part One

She was usually a very positive person. Or at least a person who could find humor in almost all situations. She made others laugh, even at her own expense at times. Some people thought she had a strong personality, but anyone who stopped to think about it would realize how selfless her behavior really was.

Her humor hid a lot of pain. She'd grown up very poor. Her father was around, but he could never hold a job. He preferred day drinking to day jobs. Her mother was a good mother, but the stress of poverty was too much for her. She slipped in and out of depression for decades. Her mother and brother had a conflicted relationship, which she saw play out with screaming and physical abuse. At first it was her mother slapping and punching her brother. As they got older, sometimes it was the other way around.

She learned to go into herself. She learned to put on a mask. Her mother didn't notice, didn't notice that she grew up, didn't notice that she quickly became the more mature and emotionally stable of the two, didn't notice that her daughter had learned how to handle life's ups and downs in much better fashion.

She applied for loans and went off to college. They were still poor, and she'd never had access to money, so she didn't think clearly through the complexities of how much she needed to borrow and how much she could do without. When she was offered a loan that allowed her to work on campus, being put into a category that made her very interesting to employers, no one told her it was because her employer would only pay her twenty-five cents on every dollar. Her loan would pay the other seventy-five cents. She didn't realize until it was too late that all her hard work was being financed against her future.

She was smart but still got a degree in the unappreciated field of education. She made an additional mistake by earning a higher degree—rarely a good investment in that field.

Before long, she found herself on the grindstone. She was working full time and eventually got a second job at the local community college. She made sure to enjoy both her jobs, since focusing on the fact that she was working eighty hours a week and still barely making enough to pay rent, a car note, her student loans, and living expenses would bring her down into a dark place. Possibly even a place as dark as her mother had been living in for so long. So she pushed on and let herself cry in the car on the dark nights while driving home from her second job.

This continued for a decade, into her early thirties. She was starting to get tired, living on the endless treadmill of the

"Working Dead." She'd coined that term. It stood for the people who worked hard and could pay their bills but couldn't save, couldn't afford a vacation, and could never afford to stop.

She did have a good place to live. She'd bought a house right after the market crash caused by the Greedy Rich. She thought she was making a good decision, buying low with a low interest rate. But she almost immediately got a pay cut, as many public employees were getting at that time. Then, even though she had a fixed interest rate, within six years her mortgage payment was $140 more a month than when she bought, because her city continued to access the property values at higher values, even as prices for homes plummeted. They had to make their revenue somehow.

But she could no longer afford the house, even with her second job. She got a roommate. That wasn't enough. Eventually, she had to make a decision: declare bankruptcy or rent out the house. She decided to make the "right" decision. She rented out the house, getting just enough to cover the mortgage but not enough to put back for maintenance or emergencies. She pushed thoughts of "what if" to the back of her mind and pressed on. She was healthy. She had a job. Life was good. She found an okay apartment in a good neighborhood. She paid more than a quarter of her income for the apartment, even while most of her neighbors paid very little to live there—as her state was so poor that almost every apartment complex accepted Section 8. Apartment complexes often raised their prices above fair market value, so they could get more money from the government for their low-income tenants. Her state had one of the highest rent-to-income ratios in the nation. Apartment owners made money off the government and off those sorry souls "wealthy" enough to pay full price for their rent. She lived there happily for several years, just praying nothing bad would happen at her house.

And then she met her future husband. He was smart and kind, and he was not part of the Working Dead. He represented everything she probably should have done. His parents could have paid for this college, but he still used two years of a four-year degree to earn a six-figure career—no student-loan debt to mention.

After a few years, he encouraged her to have faith and quit her second job. He convinced her there would be a safety net. She was fearful that the safety net was him, because she knew better than to depend on someone else. She'd learned she had to be not only her own support system but also the rock for her entire family.

So she was hesitant but eventually let herself trust. She quit her second job. She had more free time, but she immediately went into emotional debt. She couldn't pay her student loans without his help. He gladly and willingly helped. He was a good person and hadn't grown up in poverty, so for him it was just a monthly payment. To her, it was a leash around her neck, guiding every step of her life.

This went on for years, the river of life flowing quickly by as it often does.

Not perfectly smoothly, though. There eventually was a problem at the house she rented out. A toilet backed up, and her tenants tried to solve the problem themselves—with five bottles of Drain-O and waited to call her for over twelve hours. By the time she called a plumber, the entire bathroom and hallway had been flooded. She had to pay her $1500 deductible and forever declare she'd had a water emergency and had a plumbing issue on selling documents. She also realized that her tenants had severely damaged her house. She and her boyfriend made the tough decision to move into the house, even though the neighborhood had really declined since she'd moved out. They decided that love would see them through, and they moved back in. Again, life pushed on.

Eventually, they decided to get married and have a child. They were excited and nervous, as new parents are. They decided they needed more room than the modest house afforded. She'd owned the house for seven years. They should have made a profit. They didn't. They didn't even break even. The economy in her state never recovered, so neither did home values. Even after seven years, they lost $10,000, with the house selling for $20,000 less than she'd paid. He had to pull $10,000 from his retirement account for them to leave the bad house in the now-bad neighborhood.

At exactly the same time this was happening, their country was in the throes of the most ridiculous election ever. Weeks before he liquidated a fifth of his retirement to sell a house that lost value because of rich stock brokers speculating against the American people, one ugly, hateful, rich, manipulative candidate for president refused to even defend his scam to use a business loss to avoid paying taxes for years. They were regular, middle-class citizens and were not able to do the same. They couldn't claim the loss on their house on their taxes. They had to eat it.

And to make things worse, their marriage had financial consequences for her student loans. Her payments tripled and ended up being more than an entire paycheck. Day care cost over half of the other paycheck each month. She brought home less than $400 per month after student loans and day-care payment. It became even less when they added in gas. And medical bills. And boy, did they have medical bills!

Even with insurance, they owed almost $10,000 in medical bills for the birth of their daughter. They paid $1100 a month in insurance premiums and still had $10,000 in bills. And high prescription costs. She was healthy, but she had asthma. Her inhaler rose in price from fifty-five dollars to eighty dollars per month early on in their relationship. She called her doctor and asked her to prescribe the cheapest inhaler possible, effectiveness be damned. Even that less effective inhaler cost forty-five dollars per month. She rationed her inhaler, taking it only once a day to save money. Six months after her daughter was born, her inhaler shot up to seventy dollars per month. She started rationing even more, taking the inhaler only once every other day.

She had to return to work after just twelve weeks of maternity leave in order to keep in her insurance. She put her daughter in a good day care, which cost her more than a fourth of her income, even while most of the other parents paid almost nothing, because again, most people couldn't afford it. So the day cares did the same thing the apartments did: charge more so they can get more from the government, and those who could pay some would pay much.

Around the same time, a major bank admitted they defrauded millions of customers by opening accounts and applying for loans in their names. This harmed these people. The company was embarrassed. They were fined, which justified them in laying off thousands of blameless employees. But they were not forced to pay retribution to their victims. They were allowed to continue in business. And no one was sent to jail. The politicians supported this. The bank was "too big to fail," they said. They had said this about Wall Street when they destroyed the economy and wiped out billions in people's personal savings all those years before. What the politicians really meant was that the banks had contributed to their personal and private lives, and Congress had to be faithful to their donors, if not their constituents.

Her daughter got the (apparently) regular first-year-of-day-care illness, costing them hundreds of dollars in copays, labs, and prescriptions. Sometimes they paid the equivalent of her entire effective bring home of $400 on medical costs.

She started to despair. She started to slip into a hole. She wanted to contribute to her family, especially if she wasn't able to be home with her daughter. But they couldn't escape her financial past. The hardest part was seeing her normally positive happy husband start to see the world the way she did. He made good money, but she was turning him into the Working Dead. She told him he'd be better off without her.

And while all of this happened, the unprecedented election rolled on. Eventually, the ugly, hateful, rich, manipulative candidate won and was elected president. He was openly bigoted. He was openly sexist. He joked about sexual assault. He bragged about cheating people in financial deals. But he also promised to fix health care (except for women), saying he was very good at negotiating. He seemed to not be as interested in helping people as he was in proving how wonderful he was. He was untraditional. He didn't fit either major party or even the third party that had put up a candidate onto the other side. There was a major battle to see who would represent the other side. The most promising candidate—the one who had actual, intelligent plans to fix the student-loan mess, to improve health care, and to invest in the future—was railroaded. The people were cheated out of an amazing candidate. But even the backup candidate had some good ideas that would help the majority of people. And she was much smarter than the ugly, hateful, rich, manipulative candidate.

The man didn't fit with the normally rich and exclusive other side, but they adopted him because they knew he was too stupid to be anything but a rubber stamp. He won. He won the election and immediately started to harm the very idiots who voted for him—and everyone else.

They created an "improved" health-care plan that forced millions of people off the insurance rolls, because they couldn't afford it. They allowed the insurance companies to control everything. Now insurance companies were allowed to consider many basic things as "extras" and charge Cadillac prices for the plans that carried these "extras." Extras such as pediatric care, prescriptions, maternity care, labs, preventative care, and many others.

At the same time this was happening nationally, she was getting ready to file her taxes. Taxes were easy for him, but he'd never seen anything as complicated as her tax life, what with the loss on the house and her student-loan debt.

If they filed together, and got all the marriage and child benefits, her student-loan payments would stay obscenely high. In order to keep her payments manageable, they had to file separately, losing all the

Marlys   25   Addison

marriage and child benefits. With no tax shelter for them. She realized the middle class must pay for the hardships and mistakes of the lower class and to generate the ability for excess of the upper class.

Marlys   26   Addison

Part Two

It all hit at once. She had always been a liberal. She had always been a democrat. Even though her family had created the less-than-great childhood, she always understood the outside pressures that got them there. She had empathy and enough sense to understand that she didn't know everything.

But she was losing that compassion. She was losing her focus. She was finding it more and more difficult to remain positive. On the way to drop her daughter off at the day care one day, she started to cry. She wasn't entirely sure why she was crying, but she just knew that her life would never change. She was almost forty and had at least twenty-five years left of student-loan payments. She realized the money she was paying to her own loans was preventing her from saving for her daughter's college. This, she realized, is how the cycle of lower middle class continues. As a teacher, she totally understood about the cycle of poverty, but she'd never realized that even though she'd gotten out of the poverty her father created in her life, she would not be able to get her own daughter completely out. And if, heaven forbid, she and her husband broke up, she and her daughter would be right back in poverty. She had not worked so hard to be this stuck, to be this close to where she started.

Marlys   28   Addison

She felt her face and body getting hot. She noticed her hands clenching the steering wheel. She heard a guttural groan emitting from her throat. She found her hands pulling violently at her hair and forced her hands back to the wheel. She drove a bit further but then felt a nearly uncontrollable urge to slam on the breaks. She restrained herself but then realized she was gunning the gas. She needed to get some control. Her tears stopped.

She dropped off her daughter at the day care. After that she double-checked her life-insurance policy on the app for her insurance company. Then she got onto the freeway.

She drove east.

Marlys   29   Addison

Marlys   30   Addison

Part Three

She texted her husband but wouldn't answer his phone calls. She told him that she loved him and their daughter and not to worry. But she wouldn't tell him her plans. Partly because she wasn't totally sure herself but also because he was a good man, and she knew he would alert the authorities.

She continued east.

She drove west only once, and it was really more southwest. She emptied her bank account and bought a cell phone with prepaid data, minutes, and texts. Even though she hadn't started with a plan, she was smart, and a plan wasn't difficult to come by. She wanted them to wonder if she'd headed to Mexico. But that wasn't her

Marlys   31   Addison

final goal. And really she only needed a few days.

She continued east.

***

She stopped in a medium-sized city, where she had a cousin. This cousin was a nice enough person and very smart, but he was constantly underemployed. Had been underemployed for years. He didn't have a career because even though he was smart and even though his parents would have paid for his college, he refused to go. He pretended to be angry that he couldn't find a job, and he refused to adapt, to go back to school. For years he had been skimping by on odd jobs here and there, refusing opportunities at steady work because he didn't want to go through training or be at the bottom.

He was surprised to see her, but he let her in. They were family, after all, and she had given him substantial amounts of money over the years while he wistfully waited for something that would never come.

She told him she had a job opportunity for him. She told him it was with her husband's company and that he could telecommute. She told him the pay was good but that he would have to take some community-college classes.

She expected him to consider her offer seriously. Maybe if he had even pretended to consider the offer, she would have reacted differently. Maybe she would have even gone home, taken a long bath, and had a long talk with someone who could help her see a path forward.

But he immediately shut her down. He even got agitated and annoyed that she was pressuring him to take work that was unfamiliar to him and didn't inspire him. His response extinguished the wavering light at the end of the tunnel. His inability to even consider the consequences of his refusal to work had forever gated the tunnel.

He asked her to leave. He didn't even let her finish her glass of water. She stood, and her next actions were swift. As he stood to see her to the door, she grabbed her glass of water and smashed the heavy glass that he had bought after borrowing money from her into his face.

She heard crunching, and then a deep moan escaped his throat, but he stayed standing. She whipped the glass back across his head, hitting him hard in the ear. Then she brought one more swing, this time down upon the top of his skull. He fell to the ground at the same time as the shard of glass.

She got back in her car.

***

She continued east.

She thought killing someone, which is what she was sure she had done, would have a deeper impact on her. She was a gentle soul, and aside from bugs, she didn't believe in murder. But what she'd done to her cousin didn't seem to be bothering her. She had a long time to think while she drove, and as much as she took her feelings out and examined them, she couldn't find any fear or shame. In fact, she felt slightly calmer. She felt just a tiny bit more in control than she had in ages.

She used the same "I have a job for you" excuse with her nephew when she arrived at his house unexpectedly. She wondered if this would work as well on him, since unlike her cousin, he had absolutely no skills. Did it make sense she'd come all this way to offer him a minimum-wage, unskilled job? It really didn't, but in the end, he wasn't exactly a thinker, and he didn't stop to examine her motives.

But he did also immediately turn down the job. He had some leads here, he said. He couldn't really name the leads when she pretended to be interested, and that was all she needed. She took a deep breath and looked slowly around his apartment, trying to calm herself. She didn't want to kill her brother's son, but she felt the rage that said he deserved it building in her.

As she looked around his apartment, she saw the crutches for the foot surgery he'd had. When she asked him how he managed the medical bills for something like that, he said he didn't have any. *Oh, right.* She saw his Xbox and PlayStation both sitting under a large flat-screen television. She knew the television, at least, was a hand-me-down from his parents, but the game consoles weren't. And all of it looked new enough to sell for some money. She also knew that he wasn't paying child support to his ex-girlfriend.

His apartment had the stale stink of inactivity and of a human who never left. Or showered much. It disgusted her. He was able to work and didn't. He and her cousin both hid in the category of "the poor" who deserved help, hiding under the cape of better-off, hardworking liberals who were too polite to consider *any* specific situations. To even consider that not everyone who was poor had to be. That not everyone *needed* help. No, to even consider that was to be as bad as the conservatives, who refused to help anyone.

And so her own party, her own group, her own actions had created the Able-to-Work-but-Won't poor—and she suddenly realized they were just as bad as those who would help none. They were taking the aid that others actually needed. They were selfish and lazy. They gave a bad name to those who actually needed help.

Without even really thinking about it, she grabbed one of the crutches from the foot surgery he hadn't really needed and that he got for free, and she slammed the pointed end into his crotch as he sat still in his seat.

When he buckled over in pain, she drove the same pointed end into his face.

Sure, she was done, she continued east.

***

She had never been to New England and found it as beautiful as she'd always imagined. The colors of spring exploded around her—vibrant greens, purples, yellows, and reds. She soaked in the rarity of a warm spring day in upstate New York even while she marveled that her work there that day was to bring something to an end, rather than breathe new life into something.

She had been surprised how easily she had found an address for this person. Sitting in her hotel room, paid for in cash,

Marlys   40   Addison

the night before using the data on her prepaid cell phone, she'd very easily found the address for several potential targets. She could thank the inspiring but ultimately unsuccessful occupiers from a few years before for this information. Maybe they weren't totally unsuccessful; she wouldn't be bothered if later they received or took some of the credit.

She arrived at the house, an estate really, just before noon. The buildings draped themselves lazily over many more acres than necessary. The house was huge, larger than could possibly be needed for one family. There were several buildings behind and to the side of the main house. For family and guests you don't really want to see, she presumed. And then there were the garages. She saw three two-car garages, one of which was very tall, obviously meant for an RV of some sort. Probably one of those RVs that cost as much as the average house in her poor city.

She thought that these would not be the type of people who would *RV*, as a verb. Maybe the previous owners had put that in? But she thought someone this rich would have built his or her own house. Why include it? She was lost in this thought when her phone rang—her anonymous prepaid phone.

No one should have this number. It was probably a wrong number. To be safe, she didn't answer. But the phone ringing did jolt her into action. She'd formulated a plan for most of her steps. But the further east she got, the more complicated and less likely to end in success her plans were. This had forced her to prioritize her actions. She wasn't sure this would work, and if it didn't, her journey would be over. And really this was not the step that would have the most lasting impact. Or *could* have the most lasting impact. Nothing was definite. So really she should have taken her next step now, but this action was going to *feel* the best. This person represented the group that had personally harmed her the most.

She thought of all the concern she and her husband had put into getting out of that loss-of-value house. She thought about

the struggle to pay a mortgage for a house
she no longer wanted. She thought about
how her pay went down, and she was
supposed to just feel lucky she still had a job
and could pay *some* of her mortgage. But the
people she was struggling to pay, to not
default on, were the very ones who caused
the struggle; to cause home values to go
down.

She decided she'd never gotten
anywhere good by second-guessing herself;
she got out of her car and walked calmly up
to the front door.

***

It had been so easy. She supposed
being a kind of pretty, kind of common-
looking white woman helped. People don't

cross the street to get away from that. She almost laughed out loud at the irony. A white woman who had just had her ability to judge and evaluate people by appearance let her down. The woman never would have let in a black man, but she'd let in a woman—and she and her husband were murdered by that woman!

She'd said that she was the new teacher for Mr. Rutherford (she'd used access to the property records to find the owner of a house with the same house number on a different street nearby), and of course the woman had told her she had the wrong house, but she'd be glad to help her find the correct house. She figured the name Rutherford helped a bit—the woman had probably heard the name around, and it surly sounded like the name of someone who would have a private tutor.

She couldn't believe she'd made it into the house and then was equally surprised when the woman's husband, her intended third target, walked into the room. He looked as if he was dressed to go golfing. He probably wanted to get the most out of the unusually warm spring day.

The man arriving so quickly threw her plan off a bit (and really had she *actually* expected to get inside), so she improvised and did the first thing she could think of. She jumped up and slammed a vase full of flowers onto the end of a table, creating a sharp edge. She grabbed the unsuspecting wife around the throat. She cut the woman's arm, from the wrist to the elbow on the nonsuicide side. She wanted to show she meant business but keep her collateral around long enough to finish her business.

She told the man he was a selfish pig. That he'd ruined thousands of lives, tortured millions of people who were just trying to get by, happy if they had one tenth of what this man had *after* he helped destroyed the economy of an entire country. He should have gone to jail. He should have lost everything. Instead he was going golfing.

He didn't say much, but his wife, surprisingly, did. She *defended* him. That was why she killed the wife. Maybe she was always going to.

Either way, before she left their lifeless, sliced-up bodies lying on the floor of the foyer, she forced the man to wire a half million dollars to each of several different charities. These were all charities *she'd* donated to in the past, even on her small income. Then she made him post a confession and an apology on Facebook and Twitter (obviously less extensive). He almost seemed to mean what he was saying—that he was a greedy, selfish bastard who should be in jail but would settle for donating his remaining wealth before he died. She made him name the charities and the amounts.

She knew that the charities would probably not be able to keep the money, maybe not even *want* to keep the money. It had been donated in the commission of a crime and involuntarily, but she thought a public announcement would at least make the donations plausible.

Of course, it made her actions much more public and made the next steps, finishing her mission, more difficult. But then, this entire trip had been about doing what was right.

***

Now she needed to develop a bit more of a plan. Security would be tight, especially after the media firestorm following the social-media posts by the rich con man and the subsequent discovery of his death. Murder, really.

She still wanted to make sure that her message came through, and since she felt her cover would be blown any time, she decided to capitalize on the news cycle to implant her message. There was so much noise that not that many people would notice, but some would. And afterward everyone would put it all together, and it could serve as her manifesto.

That was who she had become: a person with a manifesto.

Did that make her crazy?

She drafted her message and started priming an audience using her Twitter account that she had never used before.

Marlys   50   Addison

Using hashtags such as "Real Reform Coming," "Wait for Huge News," "Wait Until You See This," and "They'll Finally Pay Their Fair Share," while tagging different members of the hateful party in power.

She had to act quickly, but that was okay, because she wanted to end it.

***

She stocked up on supplies—snacks, water, and a bomb. She needed what politicians might call both hard and soft power. She would weaponize both a bomb and social media.

She knew that even if she made it in and was able to *captivate* her audience, the likelihood of anything she forced going through or remaining in place was slim to none. That was where her social-media campaign would come into play.

She didn't want these cowards to frame themselves as the victims. Her plan worked well for this. She also used the new change in the Internet-privacy laws, which this group of legislatures had repealed, to do some underground research. She got information that she knew she could use to control them. And with every new demand, she went to Facebook Live to announce and explain the demand and details.

Facebook should have shut her down—she expected this. And the government tried to make Facebook do this, but Facebook refused to be pushed around by the federal government. In addition, they saw the reaction her demands were having. People were debating her methods, but almost no one disagreed with her demands.

Through a series of Tweets and Facebook posts, she laid out her demands: Many people wanted Congress to have to be on the insurance plan they created for the rest of the country. But those plans were created for the wealthy, so this would not harm them in any way, them being part of the wealthy. No, members of Congress had to lose their insurance altogether. There would not be different insurance for government workers and the rest of the country. Congress members only worked part-time, so Congress members would only get insurance if everyone in the country working part-time could get insurance.

And insurance would transition to single-payer insurance.

Overall, Congress needed to live on, with the plans and tax codes they implemented for the poorest Americans. No loopholes for the wealthy—at least not the wealthy who also wanted to join Congress.

There would be no closed-door meetings any longer.

Members of Congress had to send their kids in lowest-income public school in their district or city. This would ensure that Congress pushed the best educational situations for all schools. It might even encourage Congress to consult actual educators about education plans.

Congress would do away with the Electoral College. The popular vote would stand from now on.

Election districts must be geographically logical. Gerrymandering would not be allowed any longer.

The next and this one made so much sense that only Congress couldn't understand. From that day forward, only public funds could be accepted for any campaign for government office. Some of the people would have to pony up their three dollars to fund public campaigns for the first time, but so what? For the first time ever, they would get fair, representative elections.

Marlys   55   Addison

Choices would abound. Under this system, the amazing candidate from the previous election might have really flourished.

An income-gap disparity cap would be instituted. Corporations would have two years to bring equity to the pay of their top and lowest employees.

She made these demands and publicized them as she went. She knew this is what millions of Americans wanted but that they had never thought to ask for. To *demand* it. The politicians had been so successful in convincing the people that the *others* were responsible for their problems, that the people never realized the politicians had what they *all* wanted.

Now they had someone articulating something they had never thought of, but what now seemed obvious was many people wondered how they had not thought of it before.

So this realization is what caused the immediate and visceral reaction that executives at the social-media companies noticed and decided to honor and capitalize on. They kept her live. And she was able to communicate her message. And the people responded. This was her only hope for any of her demands moving forward beyond her death in that building that weekend.

And she *knew* that she would die in that building. That weekend. She knew this was not sustainable. She knew authorities would be slowly (or quickly) piecing together her week. A cousin dead in Oklahoma. A nephew dead in Nebraska. A Wall Street crook and his wife, his beneficiary, dead in New York. As many congressmen dead in Washington as necessary. Her dead in Washington. And a double-checked life-insurance policy in New Mexico.

Armed with her research that would have been near impossible to get before the repeal of the Internet-privacy standards, she made her move.

***

It took a surprisingly long time. It lasted a surprisingly long time. Because she was nonviolent, and because her bomb could do exactly what she'd hoped, could embarrass legislatures, they allowed her to stay. They tried to negotiate. They handled her bomb as if it could destroy the careers of dozens of them; and it could.

So between her manipulative hold on legislatures and her successful social-media campaign, she was able to get Congress to draft and pass all of her demands into a bill. After a few days, some in the Congress had argued that each measure should be its own law, but she knew that makes it even easier to get rid of the individual measures. If the measures were all in one bill, she hoped the citizens would push back when they saw the measures that mattered to them at risk.

It certainly helped that she arrived with a bill prepared, having prepared it in her hotel room on the way to Washington.

And lest the people think she was only focusing on the wealthy, she made clear her feelings, her manifesto, on the middle- and lower-income communities. She did include welfare reform in her bill. But it also came with the single-payer health-care system, so people capable of working wouldn't risk losing minimal benefits by getting a job. She included free day care for all. Being healthy enough to work or wondering where your kid will go shouldn't stop someone from working. She also included funds to job train people who had jobs that were in dying sectors. She knew there were thousands, maybe millions, of people who wanted to work but couldn't for some reason or another. She added that all state colleges would be tuition-free.

But for those people who could work, or work more fully, she didn't leave much. She believed that if you can work, you should. And she felt lots of Americans probably agreed with her.

***

After it was all said and done, she wasn't killed, just arrested. She was given twenty-four months' probation and a suspended sentence.

Many people felt she got off easy and wanted to make an example of her. But those people were talked off the ledge by other legislatures who knew what she must have on all of them.

Which was nothing. Her husband was the tech guy, not her. She didn't have anything, except the knowledge that the privacy law was unfair but could open the door to ridicule and embarrassment.

She was able to return to her family. Social pressure and fear of embarrassment meant that her bill passed.

Even long after she'd left, she kept her message for both groups simple and fair: Everyone deserves basic human rights, like free access to good health care, quality education, college, and job training.

And if you are fortunate enough to have more than others, be thankful, and

don't kid yourself that you got there alone—
you probably had help you don't even
recognize. So, if you pay more so that others
have a level playing field, then that's okay.
In the long run, that helps you.

And if you are born with less or have
obstacles in your path to success, take every
opportunity. Go to school, work if you can,
be a good parent, and don't bow out.

Sometimes life isn't fair but society
should be.

They called her Robyn Hood.

Mrs. Duely

Mrs. Duely

Mrs. Duely was an icon in her tight-knit community. Even though her city was steadily growing, the area in which she lived still felt very small. There were no new office buildings. There were no new housing developments and no Walmarts. People who grew up in the area met people in that area, married each other, and raised their kids in the houses down the street from their parents. And in her thirty years of teaching, Mrs. Duely taught them all.

And Mrs. Duely wasn't even that old. She started teaching when she was twenty-two and taught in the same first-grade classroom for her entire thirty-year career. So even though she'd been retired for almost five years, Mrs. Duely remained an icon, both in and out of the classroom.

Inside the classroom she was the nicest teacher anyone had ever known. Even for a first-grade teacher, Mrs. Duely's kindness stood out. She was known to follow her students' progress through elementary school and middle school. Mrs. Duely went to graduations, and she would sit down for a beer with the parents at the local bar on weekends. Mrs. Duely walked her dogs every single night and really seemed to enjoy stopping to talk to families and parents on the way.

Mrs. Duely loved her neighborhood. She loved the mix of stately and upper-middle-class homes in the varieties common to her hometown. She admired the flat-roofed, earth-toned adobes, and even though she preferred the small casitas, she still enjoyed wondering about the layout of the boxy pueblo-style minimansions. While there were also some attractive two-story plantation-style homes, most of the homes were like her sprawling, brick ranch style.

She was glad she'd thought ahead to buy a single-story house, because as she got older, climbing stairs became more and more difficult. Not that she was old or out of shape, but she knew one day she would be, and she didn't ever want to leave her neighborhood.

She loved her neighborhood. It was quiet. There were lots of trees. Even though she was in the city, she felt as if she lived in the country. Her neighborhood had always been a family neighborhood. She had always felt comfortable being out at any time of the day or night.

But that was changing; there were small cracks in the neighborhood that surrounded Mrs. Duely's world.

Jenna

I bent down to tie my running shoes and found myself smiling, marveling at being *able* to bend at the waist. I had my waist back; heck, I had my *feet* back after having Maggie nine weeks earlier! I felt much better than I thought I would.

I'm not running much yet, I thought, but even a few miles here and there was enough right now, especially since I did most of my runs with Maggie in the jogging stroller. Add in the car seat and adaptor and I'm pushing fifty pounds up and down the running trails.

I was just happy to be outside. I loved that I get exercise; Maggie gets a nice nap in the fresh air; and Ryan, who works from home, gets some peace and quiet.

I also loved getting back into my routine. I hadn't realized how much I missed that until I started again.

I picked up the pace as I neared home. I used to love this running path. Ryan and I even bought our house in part for its proximity to this path. This path runs for five miles, between our neighborhood and an even nicer one. Originally meant as an emergency drainage system, the city intelligently added the path to create more open space. I can get on this path and run west to the tennis courts, where I like to run in the older neighborhood by the golf course. Or I can run east to a great park or even beyond to the open space. I could even run to Tramway, which boasts almost nine miles of paved recreational trails, if I wanted. And all of that protected from the city streets. Yes. I was very sure I wanted to live near this path. I used to run here when I was single, and my biggest concern, if I had one, was coming across a cat or a roadrunner and my dogs going nuts and taking me for a ride.

But things have changed. On my first run after we moved, I noticed all the graffiti. Ryan noticed it too, but he noticed it in a very new-homeowner type of way, like, "Man, this sucks. Can't we have anything nice?" But my experience working in the schools gave me a clearer picture of our problem. These signs were from an established gang, not just little wannabes. I could tell that our new neighborhood was now the home of a gang.

I didn't say anything to Ryan because I was embarrassed. I had pushed really hard to live here. He had some other areas on his priority list, but I made a strong case for our two-story mission-style adobe. So I downplayed it and just kept living life like normal, because really, who doesn't have gangs in their neighborhood? Not a big deal.

I logged hundreds of miles on that path. I got to know the neighbors and the regular walkers, runners, and the cyclist commuters. I ran past YAFL football games in the fall and AYSO soccer games in the spring at the park. I stopped and let kids pet my dogs, and I became pretty good friends with my old teacher, Mrs. Duely.

And, in fact, the first person I saw on my first run back was Mrs. Duely. Of *course* it was Mrs. Duely; I sometimes wonder if Mrs. Duely ever went home.

I waved at Mrs. Duely excitedly (or least I felt like it was excitedly; it probably looked pretty tiredly) and was happy to get a wave back. I had to smile when I saw a concerned look cross Mrs. Duely's face. I was sure she was concerned to see me running so soon after Maggie came.

I could never shake the feeling that Mrs. Duely was always *evaluating* everything around her. I hadn't remembered feeling that way when Mrs. Duely was my teacher almost twenty years ago (gosh, had it been *that* long!), but then, I was six; six-year-olds aren't the most perceptive people.

Twenty minutes later, I was huffing and puffing as I banked the hill at the end of my block, when I noticed graffiti on the stop sign. I'd seen the new graffiti two nights ago, but since then it'd entered the background. Until right now. Now it popped out at me again.

At first I couldn't figure out why, but then I saw it; the unintelligible scrawl in black spray paint now had a bold white stripe through it.

I was sure that white stripe was new. It was obvious that the white stripe meant something, and I wondered what. It seemed like it would be some sort of disrespect. But what did I know? And then I caught myself thinking about the old band—the White Stripes—and I wondered what ever happened to them.

All thoughts of that white stripe and the graffiti in general disappeared, pushed out of my mind like the poisonous carbon dioxide I exhaled with each step.

Mrs. Duely

Mrs. Duely set out two cups of tea and a few sugar cookies. She enjoyed her visitations with Jenna Pearson, even if Jenna did sometimes seem uncomfortable sitting for too long. She'd known Jenna since she was Jenna McGowen. Jenna had always been a ball of energy, even as a six-year-old.

Of course, six-year-olds are energetic, but everything about Jenna was fast. You could look at her face, eyes looking just past you, and see that she was thinking. Really *thinking*. At times she slurred her speech or got frustrated when she couldn't find the right word.

Jenna's mother, Diane McGowen, had asked her if she thought Jenna needed to be tested for special education.

"Goodness, no! Mrs. McGowen, Jenna is just busy thinking. Her tongue will catch up to her brain soon enough." She'd seen the relief flood Diane McGowen's face.

And she saw that same relief in Mr. McGowen's face when she casually brought the topic up at the local pub that weekend.

"I've seen it dozens of times; kid seems like she's going a million miles a minute. They don't stop to breathe or to focus on minor details like specific words. People think something's wrong, but more often than not, these are the ones who end up performing well; top of the class, scholarships, things like that."

What she said wasn't always true, but she thought it would be closer to true than not in Jenna's case, and anyway, parents needed reassurance.

Mrs. Duely knew that the McGowens talked about the subject, but she still wanted to take the extra opportunity to set a family's fears at ease.

And she enjoyed being that source of reassurance and was proud she could do it for so many people in so many ways.

She could be the schoolmarm, reassuring the worrying mother, and she could be the down-to-earth middle-aged lady sharing stories over a beer.

She liked that she could be so many things to so many people.

Marlys   79   Addison

Jenna

I had agreed to help Mrs. Duely organize a food-and-clothing drive. As I walked up Mrs. Duely's front walk, I thought about my conversation with Ryan this morning—about my plan to suggest to Mrs. Duely that she get a dog. I thought it might be a good idea, but we knew we'd have to advertise it as more for company than for protection. The gang graffiti was increasing, but an alarming development was that there was now clearly a rival gang. My friend's husband, a cop, told me that when a gang crossed another gang's sign out, it meant they were essentially issuing a challenge. Such as "I mark you." A calling out. And at the worst, a death threat.

This was a bad development because even the stupidest little punk kid who isn't really gang material (which was what I was hoping was the case with our neighborhood) still has pride and a stupid switch.

I was surprised by how concerned it made me. I think part of it was because now I had Maggie. I had transitioned from just worrying about myself and my dogs to worrying about another human. I had to be careful for her, make smart choices. I wouldn't take the same routes near fast-moving traffic (although our posse of runner, running stroller, and two dogs was pretty big for that anyway). But I also wouldn't run as late as I used to. I used to find the dusk-to-twilight part of my run, returning home, very peaceful, enchanting. Now it was, "What if I trip?" "What if we hit a pothole" (that wasn't there forty-five minutes ago)? "What if we run into these stupid kids doing all this tagging?"

Ryan was all too happy with my increased vigilance. When I kept insisting on running at night after we heard gunshots for the first time, he tried to adopt a pit bull. A pit bull. He thought maybe three dogs, one being a pit bull, would deter any problems. I thought a pit bull would never be able to do the mileage, and three dogs on a run bordered on the absurd!

So, no, no pit bull. But I did buy a brighter headlamp and blinking reflectors to replace my reflective vest, and reflective leg bands for the dogs. Ryan was worried about a gangbanger hurting us, and I really had to fight the urge to inform him that all that we were doing was making me easier to see. But I refrained and even started moving my evening runs to the mornings, especially in the winter.

Mrs. Duely

Mrs. Duely enjoyed having Jenna Pearson visit. She knew Jenna didn't *really* want to be there. Her smiles were slightly perfunctory and not nearly as bright as when Jenna was looking at her little Maggie.

Not that Mrs. Duely felt volunteer work was as wonderful or rewarding as time with one's baby, but when she was a young mother, she'd understood that volunteer work eventually had a positive impact on her own children.

That was even truer now that their city was becoming more and more dangerous. Even their little hidden jewel of a neighborhood was being infringed upon more and more.

Sirens pierced the night regularly. More and more often, Mrs. Duely passed rough-looking people on her walks—people who were walking out of *need*, not desire. No, these people were walking as a mode of transportation.

It concerned Mrs. Duely. She didn't understand why it shouldn't concern everyone, especially those with young kids.

Which is why she pressured Jenna Pearson to volunteer for this clothing-and-food drive. If the needy families in the area could get help with things like food and clothing, then they could save that money and help themselves move up in the world. Maybe work less, which would allow them to spend more time with their children.

Which might keep their children on the right path.

Because in the end, the kids were what concerned her. Mrs. Duely saw the gang signs and knew it was the kids doing it.

And she knew that a lot of the kids were harmless. But not all of them were, and those serious ones served as an example for the others.

People the world over follow, no matter how harmful the guide. That's why Mrs. Duely was so committed to helping families. She knew if parents could be home, most of them would be great guides for their little followers.

She had to stop the bad guys from claiming her neighborhood, no matter the cost.

Marlys   87   Addison

Jenna

I was out for another early morning run, despite Ryan's hemming and hawing. I thought his concern was so cute—no one nefarious is awake at 7:00 a.m.

And I was partly right.

It was the first day of winter break, and I felt *free*! To celebrate, I slept in and started my run at 6:30 a.m. instead of 5:00 a.m. The sky was that beautiful light blue of presunrise in a town where the mountains hide the sun but still give us a hint of the warmth to come.

As I rounded the corner out of our neighborhood, I saw a figure standing over the arroyo, looking down. I was surprised to see it was Mrs. Duely. It seemed early for her to be out, but then I figured maybe this was when she walked in the morning. I hadn't seen her as much since I'd moved my runs to the early morning. I ran over to her. I arrived a bit more quietly than usual, since it was just the dogs and me, having left Maggie at home, warm in her crib.

Still, I would have thought Mrs. Duely would have heard us approach. A 130-pound runner and two dogs were just going to make a certain amount of noise. She should have heard us. But she made no indication that she did, and when I reached her, she was staring with a strange smile on her face, down into the ditch. When I followed her line of sight, I saw it. A body. A *dead* body.

I was numb. The body wasn't a body. It was a *kid*. Based on his clothes, size, and his face (how I wished I'd never seen his face), he couldn't have been more than thirteen. And it was bad. He was covered in blood, which contrasted horrifically with his bluish skin.

My dogs, sensing something wrong, started whining, and I promptly bent down and threw up what was left of my dinner. But Mrs. Duely never acknowledged our presence, less than a foot away. She just kept standing there, grinning.

I knew the kid was dead, so I called 911 and didn't go down to him, knowing all I could do at this point was interfere with a crime scene. Mrs. Duely finally spoke after I hung up with the dispatcher. She asked me if I was okay and said she hadn't meant to bother me. Then she started walking toward her house.

Shocked, I asked her if she wanted to stay and wait for the police. But she said she was cold and told me I'd be safe waiting for them alone, because I had my dogs and she thought "they" had probably left by now.

I assumed she meant the killers, but it still seemed such a strange comment.

When I was all done with the police, I went home. I hadn't called Ryan because I knew that he and Maggie were still sleeping, and this was just not something I needed to wake them for.

He went ballistic. He threatened to call our Realtor that day and called his parents asking for a loan, should we need one, to get out of the house so soon after buying.

He tried to forbid me from running from our house anymore. We both had a good laugh at that. But I did agree not to take Maggie on my runs in our neighborhood anymore. And we did get a third dog. Not a pit bull but a beautiful Siberian Husky mix. My first dog as an adult had been a Siberian Husky-Akita mix, and he had been intensely loyal, confident, and intimidating, as well as a good runner.

But I kept running in our neighborhood, so I saw the aftermath of the murder. An explosion of activity. More gang signs more often, more crossing out, more challenges. And then, within a year, two more murders. I was selfishly happy that I never saw any of those; the one I had seen was plenty. That face stayed with me. I had trouble sleeping. I became intensely interested in finding out what happened.

I found out the boy, and he was a boy, was fifteen. Fifteen. He couldn't even drive yet. He had been stabbed twenty-two times by at least four different knives. As it often goes with gang violence, the perpetrators were not exactly criminal masterminds, and they were all caught. They were all under twenty-five, one of them fourteen. They had surrounded this kid, and

in a display of teamwork that they'd
probably never been able to produce in
school, they stabbed him over and over for
fifteen minutes. Fifteen minutes is a long
time to *be* dying. Because this happened in a
nicer neighborhood, more people actually
cared about this case than usual. When
people heard this boy had struggled against
his murderers for fifteen minutes, they
called it torture and asked for the death
penalty, even though our state no longer had
the death penalty and even though one of the
murderers was fourteen. But it turns out that
these murderers were not skilled, torturous
murderers as much as they were really bad
at apparently everything they did, including

murder. They had actually been *unable* to "finish him off," as they put it.

I believed it, and I was sickened. For fifteen minutes this kid struggled and fought, in tremendous pain. The kid was a gangbanger, but he was still a kid. I just couldn't get out of my head what his last minutes on earth must have been like. Was he crying for his mom? Or was he just feeling the hatred coming off his attackers?

I still saw Mrs. Duely regularly. We still talked. She always asked about Maggie and how my classes were going.

One morning after the third murder, I got up really early for my run. I was at a crossroads. This third murder had been of a seven-year-old. It was accidental, but it was murder. The girl's older brother was in a gang, and the shooters were aiming for the brother. They missed and shot this girl as she napped on the couch after school.

The entire city was in outrage this time. It had gone too far, they said. If this can come to *our* neighborhood, where are we safe? This was actually enough to get people out of their self-absorbed little words and to care about something, someone else.

I was devastated. This girl was younger than the kids I taught. She was only six years older than Maggie. I had hardly slept that night. On top of my grief for a stranger, my grief for society as a whole, and my empathy with the parents of the little girl, I was also feeling incredibly guilty.

Ryan wanted out of this neighborhood. He felt trapped, like he was paying a mortgage every month to keep his family in a place where he felt he couldn't protect them.

Not too far into my run, I saw Mrs. Duely sitting below a sign full of graffiti, crying. She seemed entranced and didn't hear me when I approached.

"Mrs. Duely? Are you okay?" I asked tentatively. I couldn't see anything obviously wrong with her.

At first she didn't seem to hear me, but then she looked up at me, tears in her eyes and streaks down her face.

"I just wanted it to stop," she whispered.

"You just wanted what to stop, Mrs. Duely? Are you okay?"

Now Mrs. Duely broke into a full wail and cried out, "I just wanted it to stop! I never wanted anyone to get hurt. It should have just stopped it all. I just wanted them to leave, to go back to their stupid little comfortable lives and realize they were in over their heads." Her words came out in a rush, and I had a hard time keeping pace with her thoughts.

Then, I saw the can of spray paint in her hand. She held white spray paint in a lose grip in her right hand.

It all clicked in my head immediately. She'd done this. She'd brought all this down on my neighborhood.

"They were kids, Mrs. Duely! Kids! She was seven! She was seven! She was *seven*!" My words came out as hot, angry jabs. I was breathless with comprehension and anger.

She didn't have to admit it, I knew, but she did admit it.

"Go call the police; I'll wait for them at home." That was all she said, and then she walked away slowly, spray can still in hand.

A Smartass Parable on What Is Wrong with Society and Why It's a Bad Idea to Blame Teachers

Chapter One

There was once a beautiful and wonderful society that had once been even more beautiful and wonderful.

The economy was large, but it had once also been brawny enough to care for the disadvantaged. The cities were exciting, but they had once also been safe. The families were numerous, but they had once also been strong. The land was bountiful, but it had once also been pristine. The people had enough food to survive, but they had once also been healthy. The children were educated, but they had once also been intelligent.

It became clear to the people that they had taken a wrong turn in the development of their society.

Some people tried to fix the problems. Some people started campaigns to feed the poor and heal the sick. Others insisted on free services to shuttle the drunk and to protect the innocent and prosecute the guilty. Some placed pressure to return to traditions to stop the dividing and diversifying of families. Some picked a day to celebrate the Earth in all her glory, and the government instituted heavy fees to protect public lands from the public. Some people spent thousands of dollars to participate in sporting events, while others spent even more for pharmaceuticals to enhance their performance in those sports. Some people went away from their families in order to kick addictions, and some did it on television.

Yes, the people tried many different things. But none of them alone was very impactful. None of it was enough. The problems got worse. Many people decided not to have children, because the world the children would inherit would be atrocious.

The society wasn't the best anymore, and the citizens hated being second almost as much as they hated having to work to fix the problem.

So since no one wanted to do more than a little work to fix the problem, and some people didn't want to do *any* work to fix the problem, everyone eventually started blaming one another for the problems.

"It's not my fault; I'm happily married, and my mistress knows all about my wife. It must be those gays who are threatening the sanctity of marriage. Why, they don't even marry each other; that kind of behavior is why they should be forbidden from marrying each other!"

"No, no, who cares if the gays are as miserable as the rest of us? What we need to focus on is preventing the poor from infringing on my right to be rich. That's why we should force them to stop having babies and to get jobs. If they didn't have so many mouths to feed, they would be happy to work for whatever pay I deem fair."

"Well, that's fine, but what about the economy? My Sport Inutility Vehicle costs two hundred dollars a week to fill. And the granite counters I want are imported. I have to work so hard to afford all this, that I don't have time to off-road or camp in my off-road, camping-type vehicle. What we need to do is use our military power to force these terrorists and drug-dealing countries to lower their prices to cater to us. We're their biggest consumer, aren't we?"

"Damn right my dollar doesn't go as far, but it isn't the poor or foreigners' fault. We need to tax the superrich. Why should their kids be living on Easy Street without even having to go to college, while I can't afford to put my kid in college? I say taxing the rich is the answer."

And then a truly amazing thing happened. The people coalesced. They came together to speak in unison about the woes of their country. The people decided that changing themselves and one another was too difficult. So instead, they would put the hopes on their kids. This seemed to make sense, since most societies held hopes for the advancement of their young, and there existed a popular song, reminding them the children were their future.

It could have been the beginning of an amazing solution. And it was amazing because the people came together without a vote, without a spoken plan.

But had anyone looked at the kids lately, some wondered. They were a sorry group. By and large they were lazy, overweight, and mean.

They couldn't do math without a calculator, they couldn't read complex text, and they couldn't write to save their own lives, let alone their parents' lives. They didn't appear to be up to the challenge of hard work, and worse yet, they seemed to be uninterested in trying. They didn't want to step outside their comfort zone. And their collective comfort zone was dangerously small.

So the people lamented and moaned. They had a problem they knew the adults couldn't or wouldn't solve. They knew the

kids had to solve it. But the kids were ill
equipped.

They needed a solution, but the
people did not come together in a solution-
minded mind-set; they came together in a
pin-the-blame mind-set.

At first the people weren't sure
whom they should blame. So for many years
it was fashionable to blame a variety of
people. Gays and minorities took the blame,
for they were trying to change the status
quo, and certainly *that* was having an effect
on the kids.

But that didn't work well; the
connection between men having sex and
children being unable to read was difficult to

make, even for the most silly minded and hateful.

So the people moved on to blame the parents themselves. This was an interesting idea, because many of the people blaming parents were, in fact, parents. Presumably these parents were blaming *other* parents, but it was still uncomfortably close to home. In the end, there were far too many parents in the voting pool for politicians to wholeheartedly latch onto the idea. And without politicians telling them to be angry with parents, most people forgot.

But still the society declined. And blame had to be assigned. And while parents were too large and politically powerful a group to blame, single mothers weren't.

There were fewer single mothers, and they tended to be so tired from raising children that they weren't much of a political force.

But after a while, it became clear that single mothers alone couldn't be the cause, particularly because they hadn't acted alone to become single mothers. The pesky issue of the fathers kept looming. Besides, some of these single mothers were attractive, and many were young. And as can be expected in such a random population group, some single mothers were nice, and smart, and funny too. And some of the movers and shakers who decided who were out and who were in fell in love with a single mother or two. And as quickly as the fad began, it ended. It became a poor form to blame single mothers for the problems of the society.

And so, on and on it went for years, and before long, generations of people were fighting the same battle.

A sociologist would have been intrigued. Even though essentially the same problem persisted for decades and decades, each generation thought it was uniquely their own. It was almost as if the adults of one generation didn't want to acknowledge they were yesterday's failures.

People would ask why Johnny couldn't read, forgetting they had once been Johnny.

But still there *was* a Johnny. And a Claudette. And a Jerry, and a Juana. And many of them couldn't read, and most of them weren't worth their weight in T-shirts with rude sayings, expensive athletic shoes that would never be used to work out, and hooker-length shorts.

So the people still looked for scapegoats.

And then the people had a particularly rough half-decade. There were not enough jobs for the people, and the remaining jobs required more work for less pay.

And before long, people weren't looking just for explanations for why their kids were the way they were. They wanted an explanation for why everything that was wrong was wrong. They wanted an explanation for why the society was crumbling around them.

The society was hurting. There was a dull ache. A throbbing pain pulsing throughout every facet of the society.

And it was amazing because the people just transitioned. They organized like they hadn't in decades.

Some would later say they were too aligned for such a heterogeneous society.

And it was true—because they weren't thinking. They were too tired to think. The years of difficulty had taken their toll. This society hadn't really been tired, hadn't been worn down in so long that they couldn't manage it. They weren't tough enough. They hadn't had to be tough in generations.

So, yes, they were tired. Too tired to do anything but mindlessly follow.

Chapter Two

And the group that followed said the parents were at fault. And, yes, this had been tried before. But this time there was a new zeal.

The people were tired of being tired, damn it! So this time they were going to do something about it.

And do something about it, they did. The leaders of the society decided parents should be held accountable. After all, these people chose to have kids; they should be responsible for their success.

It was decided that the society should be stern but fair. They would measure how the children performed on a variety of assessments.

Since many parents already took their children to the doctor and to school, the people decided to make the tests conducted in those places the benchmark for parent performance.

Every year parents would be required to take their children to the doctor and have their height and weight measured. They would also be required to allow the local school district to measure their IQ. The data for their children would be converted into a score based on a complex mathematical equation. Parents would be ranked on a website, based on how their children performed. Some towns that were really serious about reform even printed the parents' scores in the newspaper. It was assumed this would encourage parents to try harder. Scores for an individual child were combined with the scores of the neighborhood, cities, and states to create baselines. It was assumed this would encourage the local and the state governments to allocate monies and resources to support the improvement of the height, weight, and IQ of the children.

As with the parents, the names and scores of the governments were made public.

All of this made some people uncomfortable. But when it was explained that everyone who was deemed "proficient" would receive a tax rebate, many people relaxed. Surely they were good enough parents to have their kids score in the 70th percentile or higher?

And when some argued this was inherently unfair, they were ridiculed. When the dissenters argued that many of the people making these rules weren't parents, they were told one doesn't need to be a parent to know what good parenting looks like.

And when the dissidents said it wasn't fair to rank kids based on things they can't necessarily change, such as height and weight and IQ, proponents reminded them they were ranked on whether or not the kids would be in the average range for their age. And if they were from a family that was traditionally out of that range, well, then the parents needed to modify diets, exercise, and activities to increase their odds. What *good* parent wouldn't *want* to do that?

And when complainers said that those not in range often had financial issues already, and that it was a bad idea to essentially pay those already doing well, since those not doing well probably needed the money more, the proponents argued that if parents worked hard enough in the first place, they'd get the money. And if they couldn't succeed, the government would help if necessary. They could assist with everything from plans parents could follow all the way to taking the children altogether.

That got people thinking. Worrying, really.

And then the supporters announced that not only would parents be judged on if their kids scored within that normal percentage but also every year they'd have to improve by a predetermined amount.

When complainers argued that was unfair and at some point impossible, backers ignored them.

Finally, once the plan had been in play for several years, the proponents dropped their final bomb. They announced that a parent's retirement and social-security benefits would be tied to the fruitfulness of their adult children. This was only fair, they argued. Parents used the resources of the community to raise their kids; they should produce children who would be able to give back to that community later. Tying the amount of retirement and social security— *when* they received it—to their children's earnings seemed only fair.

And for those people who didn't have kids, well, their retirement would be based on the scores of the kids in their community.

The first people to have their retirement based on their children's incomes were the next group to enter retirement age. This group had originally largely been supportive of the plan because they assumed the plan would start with the generation that had kids who were currently in school, not them. They tried to organize a protest, but they had been minding their own business so long that they were out of practice. Their protests were ineffective, and the plan moved ahead.

There were kinks immediately. This first group had children of various ages. Some parents had children as young as eighteen. Some of the kids were in college and didn't work at all. Most of those who did work had very low incomes. The retirees suffered.

So the proponents made compromises. They guaranteed each retiree a small amount and then gave them bonuses based on their children's income. This base amount was not a living wage, and those with younger children or children who didn't make as much suffered.

People argued these people shouldn't complain. But they did, because, remember, this group of retirees had protested this plan—once they realized it would affect them. They had paid money into retirement for thirty years, but now they were only being paid not by what they put in but by what their children produced.

Certainly there were many people whose children produced similar earning potentials to them. Some people never worked or worked only a few years and then their children went on to make massive earnings. Thus, they earned more in retirement.

But the much more common occurrence was for people's children to make *less* than their parents. This was due to a global economic recession and led to people receiving significantly less than they would have on the old system, which was based on what they paid in.

Some argued that the government actually planned this to save money during the recession.

The problems eventually became too much. The tide began to change.

Chapter Three

Dissent grew steadily. But things didn't change right away. As is often the case, the longer the system stayed in place, the more ingrained it became. Politicians told constituents the system had always been in place and so shouldn't change.

Finally, when an entire generation of elders couldn't pay their bills and the cost of emergency services for the newly destitute people outweighed the savings the system was making, the society switched gears.

Anger brewed just below the surface. The society needed more people and institutions to blame.

The leaders established committees all around the country—full of business executives, community leaders, parents, and even a few celebrities.

These committees met and generated some ideas. Then certain groups were designated to collate these ideas and decided on final measures.

Over many months of secretive work, rumors circulated about the committee's recommendations. The committee spokesperson always refused to confirm or deny the rumors and also refused to elaborate on their plans. And when the press provided evidence of parts of the plan that had been leaked, the spokesperson denied even the most obvious things, saying the news was utilizing alternative facts.

Finally, the committee brought their recommendations to the public.

The committee suggested that students be ranked on both their performance and the performance of their educational peers on standardized tests. Each year, students had to perform just a *smidge* better. There were many similarities between this plan and the previous plan inflicted on parents.

Only this time the consequences were student centered. A student's level of proficiency on these tests would be averaged with the average proficiency of his or her peers. Their combined scores were used to determine their placement for the next year.

This determined the classes they took and even the schools they attended.

The students with better scores were rewarded with transfers to schools with more experienced teachers and more challenging programs in neighborhoods with newer schools and more expensive curriculums and new computers.

The kids with lower scores were also placed together in schools. The goal wasn't to place them together, but it happened naturally. The real goal was to get these kids out of the schools with the high-performing kids.

It was taught these kids would pull down the higher-performing peers and even the teachers. If the teachers had to focus their energy on helping kids get caught up, they wouldn't be able to focus on the advancement of those who were already ahead.

When some pointed out this wasn't fair to those kids who were behind, the society argued that these kids were the society's best hope, and the resources should be poured into their success.

And not to worry, a plan would be created for those kids who were behind.

In addition to the yearly testing that would be used to relocate the kids, there would be short-cycle testing in reading and math.

If students weren't proficient to grade level on those tests, they had to stay in those grades until they were. The tests would be given every year between third and eleventh grades.

Opponents weren't sure how they felt about this.

At first they assumed more money would be diverted to those struggling kids, even though the government had never said it would do that. When they found out no extra money would be provided toward their education, the opponents screamed with fury.

They couldn't believe the leaders of the society would be so stupid as to hold back kids, expecting them to improve without help.

But again, the supporters of the plan thought that holding students back if they weren't proficient would encourage them to work harder to make *sure* they were proficient.

As is the nature of a heterogeneous society, many kids were *not* proficient, and before long the schools in the society were running entire programs for students who were chronologically older than their grade-level peers.

It took a while to perfect this situation, of course, and a few educational generations of students were lost in the struggle.

The younger students tended to stay in school. After all, they were as young as eight years old. However, the kids who stayed in, because they were so young, weren't always able to handle the emotions they experienced by being left behind and made to repeat grades. Behavior issues eventually became an epidemic issue. Supporters of the plan argued that these new behavior issues proved them right—these kids clearly weren't ready to advance to the next grade.

And as bad as this was, the situation was worse with the older kids. The older kids had options. At least options in actions. Many of these kids were old enough to drop out, whether formally or informally. And, unfortunately, many did just that.

And those initial dropouts were followed by a group of poorly performing, never remediated, and newly disenfranchised younger kids. This group of kids had higher dropout rates than their peers.

Before people knew it, almost two decades had passed with children being held to the standards and consequences under this plan. The dropout rate had risen. And the cutoff for what was considered "proficient" had been quietly lowered from 70 percent to 65 percent and then 60 percent. But graduation and proficiency rates had not budged.

The society became angry again. They had set really high standards and consequences for the kids for those kids. Things hadn't improved. In fact, things had gotten worse. Surely this couldn't be the fault of the kids. At least not solely their fault.

Chapter Four

So the people went back to the mental bitching board. There was the natural pendulum of blaming the old favorites, blaming anyone who was trying to change society's norms.

But before long, the society fell to the logical next group: teachers. So far, teachers were the only group involved with kids who *hadn't* been blamed. In fact, teachers had long enjoyed a grace period from the society where they were actually respected. Respected in verbiage, if not always action. Teachers were still underpaid. Teachers were still expected to teach and work for free. Teachers were still treated as if being nice was the main part of their job, rather than expertise in a field.

But now it was decided, almost as if by a silent vote, that teachers *must* be the problem. How could they not be? Teachers spent hours and hours a day with the society's children. In fact, many parents saw their kids less than their teachers did.

The fact that over half a student's education was actually divided up between *six* teachers, not *one*, so the teachers did not spend more time with kids than most parents, was ignored. And the fact that even if a child was with a teacher for six hours, parents still were responsible for the other eighteen hours a day was also ignored.

So it was decided: the teachers were at fault. And something must be done. Every day, more and more people felt the same way. It became popular and then *logical* to think this way.

And there was not much the society had to think about. They already had two examples of how to whip groups of people into shape, two examples of how to control people. The fact that both attempts had been failures was not lost on everyone, only some people.

The society handpicked some of their favorite tactics from both the parent- and student-blame plan.

It was decided that students would still be used as instruments in the judgment of the teachers. Some argued this made sense since, in theory, they were trying to improve the students. But just like in the previous plans, there was no remediation built in to help struggling students. This demonstrated clearly to some that the goal was not to help students but to judge teachers.

Students would take both annual and short-cycle assessments to test their progress both against a set of standards and against each other. Then, teachers would be assessed how their students did.

Students' scores would be listed by the teacher at the schools, in local newspapers, on the local news broadcasts, and on school websites. Finally, student's scores were compiled and used to rate schools—given an A–F grade. This was thought to motivate teachers to both work harder and motivate their students.

Once again, if students were not proficient at certain grade levels, they were held back. And once again, there were no monies provided to remediate for those students. However, the society had learned some lessons: they only held students back in third and eighth grades. All the grades in between students were allowed to continue on. It was called social promotion.

The scores of their students, in addition to the combined scores of their school, were used to evaluate teachers each year. This, in turn, determined a teacher's pay. If the teacher's students' scores were good, the teachers would get a bonus. And all the other teachers would be motivated to try harder.

However, because the previous plans hadn't worked (because they weren't blaming the correct group at that point, of course), the society was still underperforming economically. The ensuing economic difficulty meant that the society was unable (and sometimes just unwilling) to pay the bonuses to the teachers whose students performed well.

So before a few years had passed, the bonus system turned into a debit system. Teachers would be paid a certain salary, but it would be paid quarterly. New teachers would receive this base salary for the first quarter. Returning the teachers' first-quarter salary would be based on the how their students from the previous year performed on the annual assessment.

Because it took so long for the untrained scorers found on Craigslist to score the annual assessments, the returning teachers often wouldn't know their salary for the first quarter until right before the school year started.

A teacher's students' scores on the short-cycle assessments would determine the next three quarters of salary.

And here was the big change: if the majority of a teacher's students were proficient (and thus a teacher was successful), then the teacher got to *keep* his or her base salary. After all, it was a teacher's job to teach the children. Why should the teacher get a *bonus*?

And if the majority of students weren't proficient, then a teacher received a deduction in pay. Again, this was thought to be a natural motivator. And to make matters worse, teachers' base salary was based on their performance in the previous year. If they received a deduction in pay in a year, they automatically earned less at the beginning of the next year. It wasn't long before some teachers were in an inescapable rut.

One consequence (possibly intentionally) was that most teachers were making well below a living wage. But since the teachers' deducted pay was used to fund corporate tax cuts, there wasn't much motivation among lawmakers (who doubtlessly received donations from the corporations, which are people *too*!) to change any of this.

Now, granted, many teachers still made plenty of money, and in some states, the teachers even made more than a lot of people in the state. However, the majority of teachers were unable to make a mortgage-and-car payment unless they were married, preferably *not* to a teacher. And almost no teachers were able to pay back their student loans. Many teachers had second jobs and even third jobs. This, of course, impacted their focus at work. Tests scores, and thus salaries, plummeted.

Dissenters argued that this wasn't fair. That it wasn't logical. That it didn't make any sense and that, as a society, they should know better, should have already known this wouldn't work. And hadn't they tried this before, anyway?

Proponents argued that if teachers wanted to make a living wage, they must *work* for it.

But they didn't have to argue that hard. There just weren't that many people fighting against them, fighting *for* teachers. It wasn't fashionable to fight for teachers anymore. It wasn't fashionable to *be* a teacher anymore.

It was so unfashionable to be a teacher that teachers left in droves. Teaching had already had a high attrition rate. More than 50 percent of teachers left the field within seven years. After these changes, the attrition rate rose to over 70 percent in the first *five* years. This meant that very few teachers were around long enough to become masters in their field. Solutions were slower in coming, and training was constant. There were so few teachers, and scores weren't improving, so slowly some pushed to man the schools with nonprofessional, part-time instructors. The state could save on retirement costs, and districts could save on health care, but both things these part-time nonprofessionals wouldn't earn. Plus, they could be paid even less. But there was pushback against that plan from people who knew that if they couldn't dock teachers' base salary anymore, they wouldn't be able to fund the corporate-tax breaks. And even more important for the society, if the schools were manned with an army of uneducated, nonprofessional, untrained part-timers, the society would once again lose its scapegoat—because even the least rational person wouldn't be able to expect much from that group.

So professional teachers were kept on, but those teachers who stayed were sorely rewarded. At some schools, where test scores didn't improve, the entire staff

was fired and forced to reapply for jobs
nobody really wanted.

Marlys   147   Addison

Chapter Five

None of this horrible parable had been true. Of course no caring society would actually treat their citizens this way. And no intelligent society would actually be this drastic in their solutions to serious problems. And no committed society would be this wishy-washy in their dedication to solutions. So, of course, this has all been a debauched, ruthless figment of someone's imagination. Hasn't it?

About the Author

Marlys Addison grew up in Albuquerque, New Mexico, and has been a teacher for many years in New Mexico, Wisconsin, and Oregon. She has always loved to read and write. She lives with her husband, daughter, and two dogs.